Demetrius
AND THE GOLDEN GOBLET

Demetrius
AND THE GOLDEN GOBLET

BY EVE BUNTING

ILLUSTRATED BY MICHAEL HAGUE

HARCOURT BRACE JOVANOVICH
NEW YORK AND LONDON

Text copyright © 1980 by Eve Bunting
Illustrations copyright © 1980 by Michael Hague

Printed in the United States of America

LIBRARY OF CONGRESS CATALOGING IN PUBLICATION DATA
Bunting, Anne Eve.
Demetrius and the golden goblet.
Summary: A king with a passion for the ocean
requests a poor sponge diver
to describe what lies beneath the sea.
[1. Kings, queens, rulers, etc.—Fiction]
I. Hague, Michael. II. Title.
PZ7.B91527Dg   [E]   79–14865
ISBN: 0–15–223186–2   ISBN: 0–15–625282–1 pbk.

Set in VIP Palatino

First edition
B C D E

To Fred and Yolanda with love

Above all things, the young prince loved the sea.

Each day he went with his servants to the cliff that overlooked the ocean. There he sat on a furl of cushions beneath the scarlet silk of his tent and watched the village children play in the roll of the jade green waves below. Then the prince, too, seemed to feel the cool spread of the water, the surge of the white foam as it carried him, weightless, to shore.

He liked the sponge divers best, their brown bodies falling into the sparkle of ocean, pulled down, deep down, by the weight of their diving stones. The prince would hold his own breath then, the sea glimmer all around him, knowing the bright flash that came when the diver's body shot up again into sunlight. Sitting under the glow of his silken tent, he'd toss imaginary water from his hair. He'd rub the sea image from his eyes.

"Does your head ache?" a servant would ask. "Is it too hot? You wish to return to the palace?"

"Yes, I am hot. If I could swim. . . ."
The prince would try to explain. But who could
understand? Not his servants. Not his parents.

His father, the king, raised his bristle of eye-
brows. "You want to bathe in the ocean? But riv-
ers empty into that sea. In them there is dirt.
Disease."

How to explain that the sea had its own im-
mense purity?

"The sea is treacherous, my son," the queen
said. "There are strong tides and hidden dangers."

"But the people from the village . . ." the prince
began, "the divers . . . they—"

Augustus, the king's adviser spoke. "They are
but commoners, my prince. You are the only son of
a king."

Augustus was young, but his wisdom went be-
yond the limit of his years. His were the final
words.

Sometimes, when the prince sat on his cliff top, fog would creep across the ocean, gathering her great gray skirts about her. Or a storm cloud would hang like a black blister over the waiting sea. There were other times when the blueness was all a-shimmer, when every fish had its own color, and fingers of green weed waved to him, beckoned to him.

There came a night when the sea moaned and cried and called out to him to come, and the prince could resist no longer.

While the palace slept, he arose and crept past his dreaming servants.

The gardens lay patterned in silver and gray under the light of the moon, and when he looked from the cliff's edge, he saw that the moon's twin floated below on the purple sheen of the sea.

The prince held his sleeping robe high and ran down the crumble of path. Now the sea touched his feet, spun webs of foam on the shining sand.

The sponge divers' boats were shadow shapes that slept in deeper shadows.

What if he wakened one? What if he pushed it out, rowed himself along that golden path that shivered along the ocean?

But the boats were heavy. He was struggling with one when a voice spoke, frightening him.

"It's a soft night, my son, and fine for sea watching."

The prince stared into darkness and saw that a man was seated in the boat's bow. Starshine haloed his silver hair.

"Come be with me," the voice said. "Come listen and I will tell you of the sea."

The prince stepped into a patch of moonlight. Now the old man would surely know him for a prince and be shy with him and frightened in the way of all the villagers. But the man's face was turned seaward.

The prince knelt by the side of the boat and waited.

"The sea, deep down, is walled in silence," the old man said. "The blue veil opens, and you are lifted on wings of water. There are clouds of fish, shivering . . . quivering . . . and the sky above you is a liquid sky that goes on, without end, forever."

The prince closed his eyes. He clasped his hands on the boat's edge. "Yes," he whispered. "And it is like swimming through the pages of a painted book with splashes of green and streaks of silver.

"How do I know?" he wondered. "But I do know."

"There are places, hidden since the world began," the old man said dreamily. "Light spills where there is no light, and you can touch the shadows. Then you are a shadow, silent as smoke."

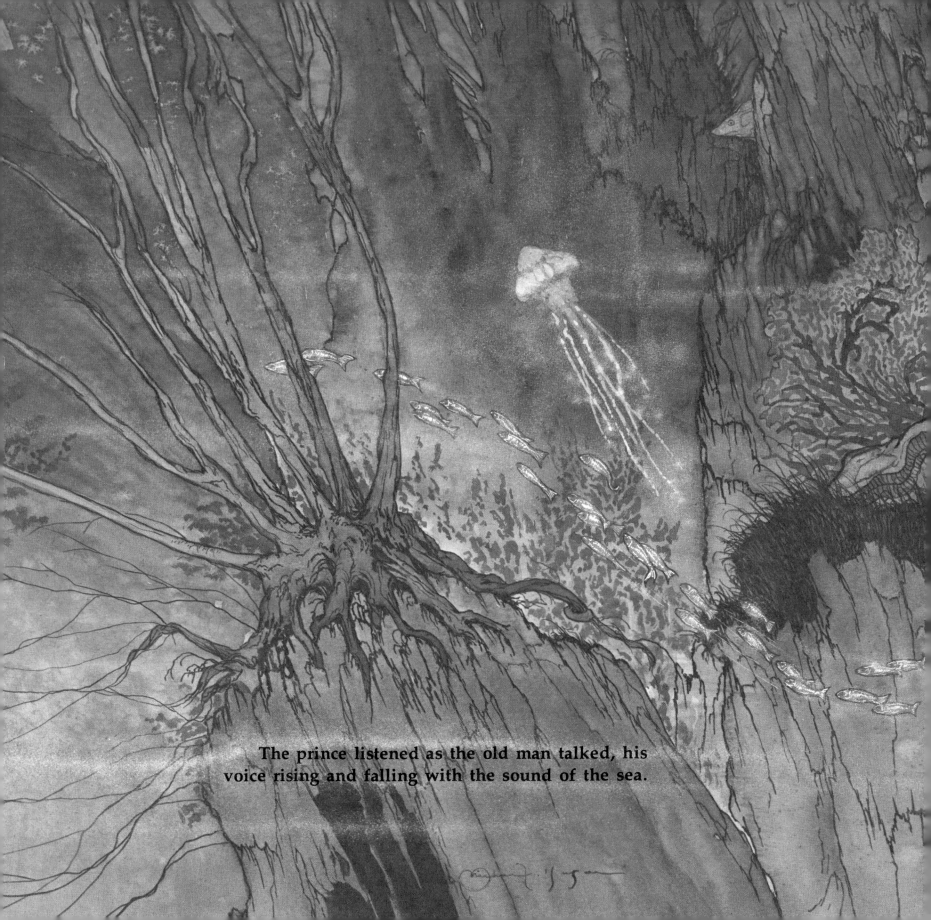

The prince listened as the old man talked, his
voice rising and falling with the sound of the sea.

Then, over the voice came another sound—a murmuring and the shuffle of slippers on the cliff path. Torch flames licked at the darkness.

"It is the king's men," the old man said. His eyes burned red in the torches' glow.

The prince stood and saw that Augustus was there and Heracles, keeper of the guards.

"There he is," a voice cried, and the prince stepped forward.

"Someone is with him," Heracles called. "Seize him."

The old man sat very still.

"It is only blind Stavros," Augustus said. "Leave him be."

"Blind?" The prince faced the old man. "You are not blind?"

"My eyes have always been without sight," the old man said. "But only my eyes."

"My prince, you must return with us," Augustus said.

"Some day we will meet again, Stavros," the prince whispered. Then, as in a dream, he walked with Augustus. As in a dream, he heard his words.

"We seek only to protect you, my prince. Because we do, I must tell the king of your journey this night."

"Blind?" the prince murmured, unhearing. "Is he truly blind?"

But Augustus did not answer.

The king sent for the prince the next morning.

"My son, it worries us, this passion you have for the ocean. Augustus has told us of last night. You must give me your word that such a thing will not happen again."

The prince put his heart in his eyes. "But . . ."

"Your word," his father repeated.

The prince saw the worry on his face and answered, "I give you my word."

"Good. But we, too, will give. I have decided to make for you your own ocean. It will be a pool

set in the rocks, bigger than any pool known to man. I have brought a craftsman from Athens so skilled that he can create the rise and fall of the tides more perfectly than the ocean itself. It will be the same, my son. But clean. Safe. An ocean fit for the son of a king."

The workers toiled for many months. Stonecutters split the rocks. Men passed baskets of earth, one to the other, along the cliff path and scattered them below. Gem cutters furrowed the sides of the pool and set them with sapphires and topazes

that gleamed wild as the eyes of great cats. Coral was taken from the ocean floor and its bite filed away. It lay in a smooth, pink ridge, and rubies hung from it, thick and red as berries on a stalk. When all was finished, great pipes poured the sea into the waiting emptiness.

"We had thought to bring fish," the king said, as the wave maker set the first wave to rippling. "But fish would soil our water. We will have pool watchers by day and by night to see that no harm touches you. Now, my son. Here is your ocean!"

The prince attired himself in his bathing dress and stepped into water as high as his shoulders.

The queen smiled down from where she stood. "You are happy, my son?"

"Very happy." The prince put his face into the blueness and saw the coral glow and the ruby fire. Then he dove down to the bottom.

But no blue veil opened before him. No clouds of fish swam past him. No light spilled where there was no light. And when he looked up, he could see, not a sky made of water, but the anxious faces of his parents.

Quickly he swam to the surface, the salt of his tears mingled with the salt of the water.

Daily and dutifully he visited his pool. Often he thought of blind Stavros.

"You have been good to me, my father," he said. "One thing more I would ask. May I talk again with the old man?"

"I will think on it," his father said.

When his answer came, it was no.

"He is a strange creature, I'm told, and his passion for the sea matches yours. It would be foolish to feed your yearning with his. Be content with what I have given you."

So the prince dreamed his dreams, bathed in the full emptiness of his pool, and turned his eyes from the glitter of ocean below his cliff.

As the years passed, the king and queen grew feeble with age. And when the time came that they died, the prince mourned them with all his heart. They had given him a lifetime of love, and their every thought had been for him and had sprung from that love. But now the prince was king.

"I am my own man at last," he told Augustus. "While my parents lived, I respected their wishes. But I swear to you, Augustus, the very blood that flows through my veins is made from sea water. Now I will do what I have always wanted to do. I will dive into those deep, dark depths. I will see for myself."

Augustus bowed low. "Sire, you are less your own man now than you ever were. A king belongs to his people. That sea where simple fishermen spread their nets is not worth risking the life of a king."

"Bring blind Stavros to me then," the king said. "For I am king now, and on this at least I will have my way."

But Stavros had died years before. His house lay empty, the messenger said. His bones were at rest in the churchyard below the hill.

"He will hear the sea there," the king said softly to himself.

Again he took to sitting beneath his scarlet tent.

"I have decided," he said one day, "That if I cannot go in the sea, I will go on it. Build me a boat, Augustus."

And a boat was built, strong enough to go in deepest water, true enough to hold the life of a king.

Each day, when the rowers had taken him a distance from shore, the king would order them to ship their oars, and he took what comfort he could from the great pulse that beat beneath the boat's hull. He'd close his eyes and feel himself one with the rhythm of the ocean.

Hungrily he watched the sponge divers.

There was one boy, quicker, surer than the others. Once he waved his captured sponge triumphantly at the royal boat, where the king sat in his royal chair.

The king's hand trembled as he set down his golden drinking goblet.

"That boy!" he said. "That diver. Bring him to me."

Augustus snapped his fingers, and the rowers rowed toward the boy in the water.

"Tell him to bring a diving stone," the king said. "Today he will dive for me."

Augustus snapped his fingers again, and the boy was pulled aboard to kneel at the feet of the king.

"His name is Demetrius," Augustus said. "He is eleven years old."

The king leaned forward. "I have seen you dive. Tell me, Demetrius. What lies under the ocean? Tell me in detail that I may close my eyes and see it for myself."

Demetrius clasped his hands about his knees to still their shivering. "Sponges grow under the ocean, and I sell three for two drachmas if they are large, and . . ."

"How do they look when they grow, these sponges?"

"Like . . . like sponges, sire."

Augustus frowned, and Demetrius stumbled on. "I have not gone down far, sire. I can hold my breath for only ninety heartbeats at best, and I hurry to find my sponges and pluck them free and come back to where there is air."

"Ninety heartbeats!" The king lifted his goblet and twirled the stem between his fingers. "The things one could see in ninety heartbeats. Tell me, Demetrius."

Demetrius curled his toes against the warm wooden planks on the bottom of the boat. One hand sought the curved comfort of his diving stone. "I go down very fast, sire. And it is shadowy below."

"Is it like going through a blue veil? And when you look up, is the sky made of water?"

Demetrius nodded and lowered his eyes as the king rushed on.

"Are you walled in silence there? Is there light spilling where there is no light?"

Demetrius nodded again. "You . . . you have been down, sire?"

The king fell silent, then shook his head as if coming out of sleep. "I was told once on a night when the sea held the moon and a tremble of stars.

. . . I have almost seen. And today, Demetrius, I will see more. *You* will be my eyes." He stood so quickly that the boat rocked. "Here is something to urge you to deeper depths than you have seen before." He held up his golden goblet. The sun plucked fire from the gems embedded in the gold, and the gold was soft looking and mellow as candle wax. "It will sink quickly," the king said. "Bring it back and it's yours. But you must tell me all that you see and think, for it is on these images that I must build my dreams."

Demetrius rose. Droplets of water from his body dripped in black splotches on the bottom of the boat. He picked up his diving stone and cradled it in his arms. His face was upturned toward the golden goblet.

"Are you ready?" the king asked.

"Yes." Demetrius took a deep breath.

The goblet made streaks of yellow and red as

the king threw it high and straight in the air, a comet, trailing its own light behind it against the blue of the sky. Then it fell, breaking the sea's surface, and its splash and the white splash of Demetrius came together, and together they disappeared.

The king lay back in his chair and closed his eyes . . .

The diver would be dropping now through the limpid blueness, and there would be no weight in him but the weight of the stone in his arms.

Long, noced butterfly fish would make a curtain of orange around him. An octopus would change from green to brown, melt into a rock as he drifted past.

The king saw Demetrius's breath rising in pearl bubbles, and he thought of the boy and how his mind would be counting off the heartbeats of air that he had used and how many were left in the fullness of his lungs.

The golden goblet would be an arm's length below now, twisting, turning. There would be coral ridges, real coral, crusted with red Gorgonias and purple sea urchins. Blue starfish would spread themselves against the living rock. He might have dropped his stone by now. He'd feel the beginning of the warning pain in his chest. . . .

The king opened his eyes. "How long?" he asked Augustus.

"Forty heartbeats, sire."

The boy would know. The king imagined him, his hair drifting soft as sea mist, a loggerhead turtle swimming beside him. A jungle of kelp moved gently in the swell. Rock cod watched from their shadowy holes. He could see it all. And the searing was in his own chest. He swam through a fog that was in his eyes and not in the sea. He was Demetrius, and he knew that he had to turn, push upward now, or he would surely die.

Then through the fog he saw the quiet shine of gold.

The goblet hung, swaying gently on the mast of a sunken galleon, the mast bleached like old ivory and twined with Neptune's lace. The jewels winked through the gloom of the moving sea.

The king stretched his hands into the heart of the waters and they closed on the goblet, and his body arched up, reached frantically for life.

Above him was liquid sky and stained-glass light, and he followed the path of his own breath to the sun. His lungs were on fire. He gasped and shook water from his hair the way he used to when he was a boy, under the swirl of the scarlet tent . . .

"Demetrius?" he whispered, and he looked and saw hands helping the boy into the boat.

"Ninety-four pulse beats," Augustus said.

Demetrius lay face down on the bottom of the boat under the envious eyes of the rowers. His hands clutched the goblet, and he took great gulps of air.

"Well?" the king asked at last.

Demetrius sat up and cradled the goblet. "I have it, sire," he said and smiled.

The king stood over him. "What did you see?"

"I saw, I saw . . ." Demetrius stammered. "I saw the goblet, sire, always below me. It twisted and turned, and oh, sire, it fell so quickly that I despaired! I reached for it and I reached for it, and it was gone."

"But what did you see?" the king asked. "Did you see what I saw?"

Demetrius stared at him with fear-filled eyes. "I saw the goblet."

"What did you think, down there in that secret silence?"

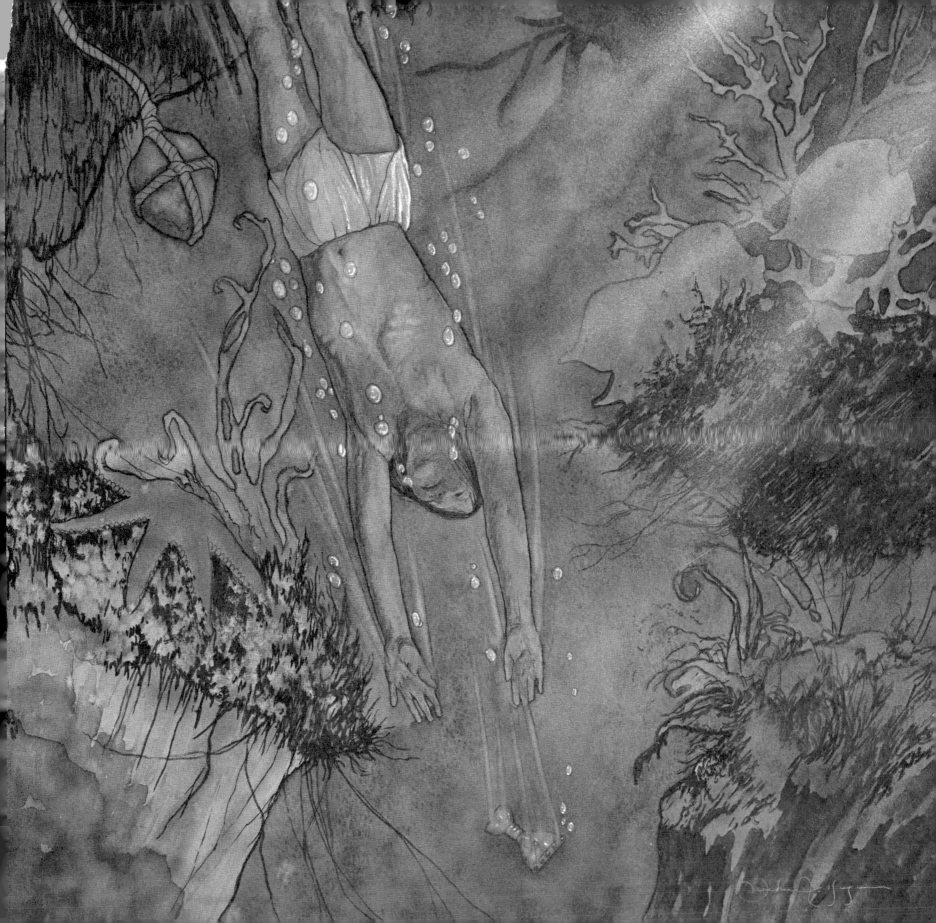

Demetrius traced the gleam of the jewels with a shy finger. "I thought about my father, sire. The money from the goblet could buy him a strong boat to carry him to where the fish lie. I thought of my mother and that she could have two milk goats, maybe three, and that there would be a new roof for our house. Our roof has not kept out the rain for many months and . . ."

Rough hands pulled him up.

"You went on a mission for the king!" Augustus said angrily. "You failed him. The king has learned nothing from you, you worthless boy." He cast the boy aside.

The king stared across the ocean. "Tell me, Demetrius. Did you find it at the end hanging from the ivory mast of a drowned galleon? Was that where you found it?"

"Nay, sire. It was stuck in sea slime, or I'd never have had it."

"Sea slime!" The king smiled. "It is not true, Augustus, that today I have learned nothing. I

He lifted his hand, and the rowers turned the royal boat and pointed it toward shore.

have learned that the heart sees more clearly than the eyes will ever see. It is a lesson I should have understood a long time ago. Once I had the wisdom to know that the sea's secrets cannot be held in a jeweled pool. Today I learned that neither can they be carried back in a golden goblet." He touched Demetrius's shoulder. "We will take you home now. Good health to you and your goats. May your new roof and your new boat both keep out water, and may your sea be filled with many sponges."

This book was set in VIP Palatino by Connecticut Printers, Incorporated.
It was printed by offset on 80 lb. Patina supplied by Lindenmeyr Paper Corporation.
The drawings were done in India ink, watercolor, and gouache.
Separations were made by Capper Incorporated.
Printed by Pearl Pressman Liberty.
Bound by Economy Book Bindery.
Designed by Barbara DuPree Knowles.